PRICK

PRICK

THE HANSOM HUSTLA

PALMETTO
PUBLISHING
Charleston, SC
www.PalmettoPublishing.com

Copyright © 2023 by The Hansom Hustla

All rights reserved.

No portion of this book may be reproduced, stored in a retrieval system, or transmitted in any form by any means—electronic, mechanical, photocopy, recording, or other—except for brief quotations in printed reviews, without prior permission of the author.

Paperback ISBN: 979-8-8229-3353-8

CONTENTS

Introduction · vii

Chapter 1 - Early Childhood · · · · · · · · · · · · · · 1

Chapter 2 · 7

Chapter 3 · 14

Chapter 4 · 24

Chapter 5 · 36

Chapter 6 · 48

Chapter 7 · 62

INTRODUCTION

It was a warm, beautiful spring afternoon. The birds were chirping and the children were playing without a care in the world. One would say it was a perfect day, perfect for everyone but me and Daniel Stanley that is. I was nervous as hell, but calm and Daniel never saw me coming. I will never forget that day because despite of all my training, I still didn't believe that I was ready. On May 16th 2002, I became a killer. Since that day I've become known to numerous people around the world simply as the plague because of my unique style of killing.

    I grew up an orphan without any knowledge of my fraternal parents. At age 17 I was literally put out on the streets due to overcrowding. I did almost any and everything to survive until one day I was recruited, so to speak, by my mentor. He was a cold plus harsh man but he gave me the family environment that I longed so much for. I went

The Hansom Hustla

through endless hours of training that got me prepared for any situation. I learned hand to hand combat, how to operate any type of weapon, how to survive in any element and especially how to suppress my emotions. I trained for five years straight until my mentor felt I was ready then, on May 9th 2002, I received my first assignment.... After studying my target for six days, (day and night) I chose my weapon and made my move.

Even though this is the only occupation I know, I can definitely say that I enjoy my work. What other job can you demand millions, never "hit a clock" and you give your "boss" a time frame and they don't hound you about completing your task? Others in my field conduct business totally different from the way I do, but not all can say that they have an 100% kill rate like I can. I choose to get up close and personal because other methods, in my opinion, require too much equipment or make too much noise. I simply study my target, approach them, then with one pick my job is clone. There's no loud explosions, no running the risk of someone spotting me pulling at a weapon, nor any innocent bystanders getting hurt. I do my job then I'm gone, in and out like a gust of wind.

CHAPTER 1
EARLY CHILDHOOD

The earlier part of my childhood is simply a blurr. I was told by Ms. Edna Burke, the older lady that ran the orphanage, that I was just left on the doorstep one morning by God know who. I can't tell you exactly when my birthdate is, but I can tell you that I celebrate it on September 16th, the day that I was found on the doorstep. All I can recall were my first days of school, I hated it deeply, that is until I met Erica. Erica flowers was an older kid that took me under her wing, she was an orphan like me so she could relate to what I was going through. Although I was stand offish to everyone else, I could feel comfortable and open up to her. Even though Erica was a few years older than I, we were the best of friends. We were inseparable for three short years, until she got adopted. She wrote me from to time but I never saw her again. I was eight at the time and losing my friend broke my heart which made me retreat

The Hansom Hustla

back to my shell. I never knew the feel of new clothes because everything that I got were hand me downs that the other girls couldn't wear anymore. Even though my clothes weren't new, it was still an exciting time to get something different to add to my wardrobe. I learned that before I came to this place it used to house boys too, that is until Ms. Burke caught a few of them taking turns with two of the faster girls that stayed there. All the boys were then swiftly shipped out across town to an all boys home which of course left nothing but us girls. After the boys left Ms. Burke ran the place like a well oiled machine. She made sure that even though we out numbered her by a great deal that none of us got out of line. Growing up in a house with all girls was rough, they can be some mean creatures at times, and since I kept to myself I was the main focus of most of the girl's lashing out. Especially one girl in particular named Iesha Jones, she was one of the biggest girls in the house, and the meanest. I won't lie, I was pretty terrified of her. She would do any and everything to me to get a laugh, but mostly just because ... you know your typical bully. Iesha was my worse nightmare until I was around eleven. Living in an orphanage meant I didn't get many toys growing up, but on my ninth birthday I received the best gift that I ever had, I was given my very first cabbage patch doll!! Oh how I loved that doll so! I named her Erica after my best and only friend, that I knew for such a short while. I took Erica everywhere with me. One day I woke up and Erica was gone. I searched high and low for her and couldn't find her, that night and a few after that, I cried myself to sleep. Three days later she ended up in Iesha's hands. I begged and pleaded for her to give me my doll back and of course she didn't. She held her so high above my head that it did nothing but taunt me. While begging I started to cry, I remember the word that she spoke to me like it was yesterday. "Aww, look at the little baby crying!" "Lol, you want your doll little baby?" "Well, here!" as he ripped Erica's head from her shoulders. I sat and sobbed deeply while she walked off laughing. In a blind rage I picked up the biggest book that I could find, ran down the hallway to the backyard where Iesha and her band of followers stood around laughing about the event that just took place and started swinging. I swung and swung until Iesha hit the ground then swung some more. When I stopped swinging I started kicking and when I stopped kicking I started back swinging. When Ms. Burke finally stopped me, Iesha just laid there in a puddle of blood, I thought that I had killed her. After my altercation, living in the girl's home got a lot easier. Iesha, nor anyone else for that matter, bothered me anymore. It wasn't until I started liking boys that my life got a little more complicated. From age eleven to thirteen I sat quietly in my corner and watched girls come and go. I counted a total of fifteen in those four years that went to foster homes. Every other Tuesday was adoption day and everyone except me got excited. They would be hustling around doing each other's hair and putting on their best outfits. Even though I was always happy for the girls that got chose, I knew that neither one would ever be me. Some

The Hansom Hustla

of the girls would cry when they saw each other go, their faces would be filled with tears and mouths with broken promises of how they were going to keep in touch, but in a couple of months those promises became untrue. I found out way back then that people will believe anything to get them through. On my fourteenth birthday Ms. Burke was able to replace my doll, but it wasn't the same, nothing nor no one at that time could fill that pain that I felt when Iesha ripped my best friend's head off with one effortless tug. My new doll's name was Carla, I drug her around just to have someone to talk to. I filled Carla in about the events of my life that she missed before she came along, how my best friend left and how Iesha ripped off Erica's head, how much I hated school and that she was the only friend that I have. We sat and talked for hours about the events of my days. Everyday Carla would see me off to school and greet me when I got home and most days it'll be the same stories just different teacher's names. Then one day out of the blue, Theodore Wilkerson approached me at lunch. He simply asked if anyone was sitting in the empty chair across from me, but it changed my life. Before that day I thought that I was invisible to everyone but my teachers and Ms. Burke, but apparently not. Theodore spoke to me again about a week later, it blew my mind that he actually knew my name and needless to say, he became my first crush. I would shyly wave to him when I saw him walking by and hung onto every word that he spoke when the teacher called on him to read out loud or ask him to answer a question from our assignments. Because I was so shy I wouldn't dare to actually talk to him, but Carla and I would go over the details of how the conversation would play out between us two. It would always end with him hugging me ever so tightly then grabbing my hand and him slowly walking me home. This conversation went on for months until one day I saw him talking to Cindy Welch, they were smiling and laughing with each other and he even carried her books to class. Deep down inside I was flooded with tears but couldn't let it show. That day I ran home after school, climbed in my bed and cried myself to sleep. Around the time that my fifteenth birthday rolled around I started getting more looks and stares from the opposite sex due to me pretty my developing "overnight". I went from a?? to a cup seemingly in a blink of an eye, but I didn't pay attention to any of them. I could never forget the pain that I felt of seeing Theodore with Cindy. My sophomore year is when all of my teachers and counselor started telling us students how important it is to go to college and now is the time that we should try to figure out what we wanted to be or do when we get older. A lot of the other kids seemed to have figured it out already while I was just trying to pass this math class. It wasn't until my junior year that I actually found a subject that I liked. I couldn't wait to get to biology class to see what else I could learn about the circulatory system and then human organs and how everything works together like a tight knit community. This type of stuff fascinated me and it's all that me and Carla talked about. Later that year I was told that I needed

The Hansom Hustla

to take the ACT or SAT to see if I would qualify to go to college and even though college was the furthest thing on my mind, I took both. As my senior year rolled around the only thing that I could constantly think about was just graduating and getting as far away from this place as possible. I was thinking that I could fixed me a job somewhere then figure it out later. My first two semesters went by swiftly. I completed all my regulated hours but still had electives that I need to pass in order to get an academic diploma. It seemed like my final semester in high school took forever, but I was finally notified that I would be graduating on time with an academic diploma. But come to find out on graduation day, that this too was bitter sweet. While everyone else had their families and even other students cheer as their names were called, not even one teacher clapped as I received the first major achievement in my life and when I finally got back to the orphanage, I was met by Ms. Burke with the worst news that I've heard in my life.

CHAPTER 2

It was a good thing that I did take those tests (ACT/SAT) while in my junior year. Come to find out, I did well enough on one of those that I was accepted to a small junior college, which was a great thing, not because of the education, but because I would finally have a place to sleep again. These last two and a half months were rough. I was arrested for shoplifting, which got me out of the rain for a few nights, my clothes were stolen by god knows who and I was damn near rapped by some other homeless dude. This was around the same time I started mastering my crafts of boosting and pick pocketing. I got so good that I didn't have to worry about where my next meal was coming from but hadn't figured out my sleeping situation until I was enrolled in Ju-co. In case you hadn't guessed it, the news Ms. Burke gave me was that she could no longer house me. Yup, the same day as my high school graduation I was forced to figure things out on my own. The first few nights went by quickly. I was scared to death of being out here alone. Being in the

The Hansom Hustla

orphanage was different, even though I am a lower, I could always retreat to my bad, but not out here. I had to figure some stuff out and fast. I tried standing at the red lights begging for change, but the longer I stood there the more men would stop asking about a "good time". I even tried begging at the grocery store with little to no luck. I was on the struts for about a week and a half when my hunger got the best of me and I walked in the grocery store with the two dollars and sixty-eight cents that I hustled up on, picked up anything that I could stuff in my small pockets and a bag of chips that I attempted to purchase but was caught by the in store security before I was even able to make it to the counter. I sat in jail for two and a half weeks before I saw the judge and was released on my own recognizance. While I was incarcerated I meet and only spoke to my roommate, Kathy Ingram, Kathy was only about two years older than I but had been in and out the system since her fourteenth birthday now at 19 she spoke and moved like a pro. We went to court together, the judge gave Kathy two more weeks to do and since I was getting out she sent me to see here people and deliver the news about court. Kathy's people were pretty cool, they let me sleep there since I had nowhere else to go. They pulled all kinds of scams to get by and if those didn't work they simply just took whatever they wanted. Since I was there with them I had to learns quickly how to pull my own weight. Meaning whatever was going on that day I had to be a part of it, especially if I wanted to eat that day. The first "mission" I went on with them was to the mall to go "shopping". I was told to look out and run interference if someone would come in that particular section. This was the first time in my short life that I actually knew how it felt to have brand new clothes, it is a memory that I would never forget. The smell of the clothes, the rush of the act, and satisfaction of popping a tag of an item had me hooked. Needless to say that I was addicted. I stock so many clothes that I actually stole some of the same outfits that twice. I found out that the black boys were always willing to pay for anything that they didn't have to pay full price for so they were my go-to guys when I had extra items that I couldn't do anything with. Boosting kept a few dollars in my packet and I hadn't missed a meal in days, Kathy got out on a Tuesday morning, by that afternoon she was teaching me how to spot someone with decent money and my first lesson on pick pocketing. We went downtown around lunch time to scope out different prospects. As we walked around seeming aimlessly about through the foot traffic of the downtown lunch rush, I saw Kathy bump into a man, argue with him for a second about watching where he was going then as soon as we turned to walk away she states that lunch is on him today and slowly reveals that she had his wallet in her hand. I kept Kathy up for a few days making her teach me how to do her craft until I could do it with almost as much case as my teacher. Starting the very next week, I would start boosting during the day and pick-pocketing at night. We did pretty much the same routine every day just different spots. It seemed like life was good for everyone else around us, especially in the spots we went to do our thing. Deep down inside I envied them because even though I was in a place in my life that I've never been, I actually didn't want to be doing the stuff that I was doing to live like I was. Despite all of that, I had to do what I had to do to make sure I could eat. Kathy and the rest of her people were discussing moving to a new city to keep from getting too comfortable or getting spotted by someone that they've ripped off in the recent weeks. This conversation lasted for about a week then on a random Wednesday morning, I woke up and everyone including Kathy were gone and once again, I was all alone. I had enough money to get me by for a few days, but I'd definitely would need to get back to work soon. The only problems that I was facing now is that I was alone. Every scheme or plot that I knew was based on haring at least two people on the job just me here would definitely be a challenge. The next night I went out on my first solo mission. I was noticeably nervous and had to walk for about a mile until I was calm enough to not be physically shaking. As I headed back towards the square to find a victim, my focus was broken from the loud sound of a siren followed by the yelling of a police officer. I took that as a sign so I slowly slipped back into the shadows and went my own little way. The clay after was a lot better, damn near too easy. My first "bump" I "lifted" a wallet full of twenties from a dude and two credit cards and another eighty bucks from this lady pulling a cart full of groceries. I was set again for a couple of days. It wasn't until a week later that my living situation started to become a problem again. The spot where Kathy and her crew left me was getting boarded up in front of my eyes. And with no back-up plan, I was roaming the streets again. It was a good thing that I was pretty good at boosting, because I needed somewhere to store my extra inventory, I got a storage unit. And that's where I stayed for a couple of days until I remembered about my Ju-co acceptance, the very next day I went to enroll. In order for me to afford school I applied for a few loans and grants. I was granted a grant that allowed me to attend school for free as long as I maintained a B average. The first semester was challenging for me I had to constantly ask questions and take notes. It wasn't until I realized that no one actually checked the library before it closed that I would start my homework in one area then eventually end up in a back room where I would stay until the library closes. This killed two issues 1) my sleeping situation and 2) me maintaining my B average. It wasn't until winter break that I stumbled onto an issue with my sleeping situation again. At this time my life consisted of class first thing in the morning, going to "work" for a few hours then retreat back to be library before it closes for the night. This was the same routine for a few months then something changed during the winter break. I couldn't put my finger on it at first, so I chalked it up as just me being paranoid. But it seemed like everywhere I went I was having the same eerie feeling ... it started the second day I was out "working" I was just about to grab a few items out of Macy's when the feeling came

The Hansom Hustla

over me that I was being watched. I got the same feeling two days later as I roamed through the square after I "lifted" this dude's wallet. And the very next day at the grocery store. By the end of the week I was certain that I would be getting arrested, but I didn't let that stop me. I would go to "work" then disappear back to my storage unit. The feeling escaped me for a week or two, around the same time that a new semester was about to start then the feeling rushed me again. As I went to "work" I choose a different type of victim, this dude was dressed down, like a tourist. I usually only targeted the business type of dude's or just locals, after I "bumped" this dude and lifted his wallet It was something on his license that stuck out, his name. For some odd reason I kept thinking who would name their child two last names? Bryant. Johnson was his name and besides him carrying around a two dollar bill, his name implanted in my head. A few days and a few spots later, I got that feeling again. As I went along with my daily route I was approached by a woman with a confused look on her face. She asked me if I was from around the area and did I know where to locate one of the more famous restaurants in the city called L.C's. I directed her to her designation and suggested for her to try the house special and the cakes are great. With a pivot to the left I was damn near run over by a jogger but I was back on my mission. A purse and two wallets later I was heading towards my storage when I heard a voice that broke my stride saying "you're pretty good at what you do, but you could use a little more practice". I looked back just for my eyes to lay upon a familiar face, it was the same face on the i.d. from the other day. "Bryant" I asked questionably he responded by extending his hand and saying "now that we've been introduced properly, you can give me back my wallet".

CHAPTER 3

I don't have it anymore. I noticed that you have two last names which made me pay attention to your picture and that's how I recognized your face. Bryant asked why I do what I do and what part of town I was staying in? I was reluctant to answer since I didn't know him and the fear of him turning me in to the police because of what I've been doing. He assured me that he wasn't going to call the police and he was just curious about what got me out here wandering the streets and doing petty crimes. I was still reserved about talking to him and I guess that he could sense that so he withdrew and let me scurry on about my way. Two days later, and my first day of my sociology class, I was shocked to notice a familiar face. I really couldn't make him out at first because I always sat in the very back of the class and his back was turned towards me, I recognized the voice as he wrote his name on the board, it was the man with the two last names. Now it made sense of why he was in the square that day. The square is usually a hot spot for tourist, but it also is known as the best place to hang out for broke college kids since it was located a block or two away from the campus. My train of thought was broken by Mr. Johnson asking everyone in the class to fill up the first couple of rows in the class. He also stated his 3 rules to the class 1) Respect any and everyone's thoughts and beliefs 2) No one is allowed to sit in any other rows past the row we're in now and 3) this one proved to be my most difficult, everyone has to participate in class discussions. He also explained that it wasn't really a lesson plan for our class because it was more of a "topic of the day" type of class, as he was moving around the front of the chalkboard I couldn't help but wonder if he noticed me, my question was answered swiftly when Mr. Johnson brought up our first topic in this class, "when is stealing justified?" My pen dropped.

After about a three minute pause the silence was broken by a clearing of the dude's throat that was sitting to my left. He began his comment by saying that he actually doesn't see a circumstance where stealing would be necessary. Mr. Johnson replied by saying that was an interesting way of looking at it and does anyone else have an opinion? This carried on for an hour and everyone in our 15 person class had stated their opinion but me. Mr. Johnson decided to dedicate the last twenty minutes of class to hearing my point of view, I started off saying well, everything is situational, he asked me to elaborate on that and just as I was about to give my example(s) to support my answer, the time was up in the class. Mr. Johnson stated that we'll revisit this topic

The Hansom Hustla

in our next meeting. And the very next week he entered the class with a comment of, we left off our conversation last week with the young lady saying that she believes that stealing can be justified depending on the situation. While looking firmly at me he asked would I care to elaborate? I Proceeded to say that sure mostly all of us, if not all of us know right from wrong, but what if it's your only means to get by? The same dude to my left quickly bursted out, then get a job! And I rebuttaled, sometimes it isn't that easy. Mr. Johnson interrupted with an Ahh!! that's the underline stuff that this class is about and how I would like all of you to start looking at things, he continued by saying, by a show of hands how many of you could afford to pay to attend here? And how many of you had or has to work their buff off to afford this? And lastly who's all on a scholarship? The point that I'm trying to get you all to see is sometime it isn't about the path you took but the designation it brings you to. I couldn't help but to drift off in thought after that statement, Mr. Johnson couldn't be too bad of an individual if he can see things from more than one point of view. I snapped out of my day dream in time enough to hear the topic of next week's conversation. Which will be, should someone's social status affect the way you view or treat them? with that question lingering in my head, I headed to my place of solitude the library.

Although I'm rather reserve, I made sure that my comments were short and to the point. So even though I didn't say much, the stuff I said was beneficial. I felt like this class was safe zone where I could get my point across without being judged. We all had an opportunity to hear each other out and open our eyes to everyone else reality. When it was my turn to speak, I started my statement by saying that I believe that the less fortunate is invisible in today's society. Take me for example, I bet that neither one of you would have actually acknowledged me if it wasn't for this class. Another female chimed in from the front row, clean, I agree. While we're in this room we all respect and recognize one another for being each other's equal, but as soon as we leave this room our version of reality kicks in, and we go back to our own little corner of the world. Mr. Johnson asked if this is what everyone in the class experiences from day to day? Most of us agreed only a few of us acted like they didn't notice it or it just didn't exist. Mr. Johnson turned towards one of the few that didn't agree and asked her what her point of view was on the subject. With a pause (just to glance around the room) she confidently said that less fortunate people make themselves invisible. Another student asked how is that so? The confident girl, Cindy, Cindy Cartmoore, replied by saying they do things like always stay in the back of the crowds or in the shadows, they do their best just to blend in, they're too worried about what type of impression they'll make so they often come off as someone else and you can tell by their body language that they don't want to be bothered like looking clown and speaking low or not talking at all. Mr. Johnson interrupted by saying Ahh! See now we're coming to the nucleus of what it is, most

The Hansom Hustla

of the class was looking confused, he continued by saying. Most people view other people by what they wear weather it be a hoodie and sweats all the time down to something that's ???????????? any of your body parts, you're going to be judged. It could be a hair-do or something as simple as your nail polish, some one is always going to have something to say. My question to you guys is, how much will you make that fact matter in you life? Is another person's opinion that important that you'll dedicate your lite to be a person you're not just for an approval or can you look at life beyond this classroom with the same open eye that you bring to these discussions? You never know how far a simple hey, how are you doing today? Can take you and/or what it'll mean to the next person who might not think or feel like they belong. With those words being said it was a type of awkward silence that fell across the room. The look and feel of guilt mixed with shame spread across the room as we were dismissed. Needless to say, this was my favorite class and also the only class that I actually was acknowledged and spoke in. The next two weeks were pretty much the same. We addressed numerous topics that kept a certain type of tension in the room, which I came to sort-of enjoy. It was the same feeling that I felt right before my first (and only) fight at the orphanage. I couldn't wait to get back to Mr. Johnson's class so we can stir the pot with one-sided comments and views. Until one day he switched the program. I had overslept and was running late to class. When I got there I was shocked to see everyone paired up and having personal discussions. What's going on? I asked and Mr. Johnson happily explained that he decided to pair everyone up and have them hang with each other for a week to see life from a different point of viewed. I thought to myself that it's a good thing that this is a fifteen person class, but he continued with, and since this is a fifteen person class and you had the luxury of being late today so guess who you'll be paired up with? I was hoping that he was joking, but from the look on his and everyone else's face that this was no joke. As much as I like this class, this has to be some of the worst ??? I could here at this time in my life.

Don't look so excited was the next thing that came out of his mouth. I was speechless, he continued by saying; well, ask me anything and I'll answer, what would you like to know? Well, how does this project work, do we call each other every night like we're besties or something? Mr. Johnson replied with an Oh!, did I forget to mention that in order for this project to completely work you guys will need to spend the next 6 days together, you can go back home on Sunday to get your report together for Monday where everyone will present what they've learned about their partners. I would like you all to spend three nights at each other's place then switch, this will help you understand what the other person has to go through on a day to day basis. I believe that part of the project threw everybody for a loop. Mostly all of us students were looking around in disbelief. In the back of my mind I was wondering how I could make this thing work

The Hansom Hustla

when it's Mr. Johnson's turn to come live with me, do I just lead him to the library and be like welcome to my humble abode or should I just come clean now? We carried on with class as if it was a normal day and as soon as the class was dismissed I was pulled to the side. Mr. Johnson told me that his last class is at 4 and I could catch back up to him here in the classroom at the end of the day, I shook my head in agreeance, but still had a many questions rambling around in my head. With all of this going on, I could only think to myself that this is going to be a tough week and headed out of the classroom.

Since sociology was my only class today, I figured I'd go get a little work in before four. I'd have to choose a different location since a lot of the crowd in the square would be somewhat familiar faces. It was still early and looked as if we'll be having some pretty good weather, so I chose to go downtown. I should be able to lift a wallet or two from one or two of the cooperate workers that's headed for an early lunch. After a lite day downtown, I decided to head back to the school a little early, I got back to Mr. Johnson's class around 3:20 or so and had on opportunity to sit in on the second half of his last class. With this class he seemed more firm and distant. Just sitting back and observing Mr. Johnson was standoffish in this class opposed to my class in which he seemed more involved and relaxed. This was a side of him that I hadn't seen, but I have seen the look that he gave a student after she so rudely interrupted him. It was that same look he had on his face when he asked for his wallet back. A look that I would encounter numerous times after that. As he turned to address the young woman, his eyes caught a glimpse of me standing in the shadows then motioned for me to sit without loosing his stern look or tune in his voice, he spoke to the young lady; "Don't interrupt my class again if you're not going to add depth to our conversation" then swiftly carried on with his prior thought. I would have never thought that he was so "stiff", he's so open with us.

After class I walked down front so we could start our project. He hardly looked up as I spoke. While fastening the buckle on his briefcase, he stores at me and says, well would you like to start our study at your house or mine? With a brief pause, and a dop of my eyes I answered yours. He motioned me to follow him, as we hurried through the halls I broke the silence by asking Mr. Johnson if he was married? With a swift "no" he bounced up the steps taking two at a time. Speaking over his shoulder at me, he started that I might want to keep up if I plan on shadowing him. He moved so smooth and swiftly through the crowd that at times make it hard for me to keep up. We made a left by the subway and proceeded up the hill. Seemed like twenty hills and four miles later we finally arrived at Mr. Johnson's townhouse. It was in need of some work and a good paint job the inside wasn't that much better. It looked as if he hadn't cleaned since he moved in Swinging the door closed behind me he said, Welcome to my house....it aren't much, but it's all that I have. He showed me around the two bed

The Hansom Hustla

two bath house, the last room be showed me was the room that I'll be sleeping in. He left me there to get comfortable and all I could think was well, at least I'll have a bed to sleep in for the next three days. The next day when I woke up Mr. Johnson was gone, he left a note on the table that said went for us run, be dressed and ready to go when I get back & breakfast is on the stove. In the process of me turning to look on the stove I heard what sounded like the back door opening. Mr. Johnson was walking through the door talking what looked like a horse. His voice carrying heavy through the halls, barking the questions Did you read the note I left on the table? I answered yes, then he followed by, so why aren't you ready? We're losing time, we need to go. I was dressed and ready to go ten minutes later, but Mr. Johnson wouldn't stop fussing about how I'm throwing his morning routine off which consisted of a two mile jog that ended at the yard where his champion mastiffs were kept, the one with him today is the baby, where he cleaned their pens, feed and walked them then a two mile jog back home to shower just to take a four mile walk to the campus in time enough to have a cup of tea before our nine O'clock class. Today he only walked one dog and was waiting for my help to walk them all as a group. He walked and fed the dogs, went to shower then off on our journey back to the campus. He was light on his feet and seemed to glide there the crowd. It was so elegante that it brought pleasure to me to see. I guess you can say that it was like watching a leaf dance in the wind on it's journey to the ground. The

PRICK

next day, and our final day of me being at Mr. Johnson's house, we took a different route home. This way seemed to be longer and fall of foot traffic. While I lagged behind to watch his graceful footwork something caught my eye. Mr. Johnson glanced back to see if I was still at to (something he'd never done by) then about a mile later he did it again. Five minutes after we walked in the house, he called me in the kitchen, I was in disbelief as to what I saw on the table. He looked at me and asked me was I paying attention to how he moved three the crowds? I should my head eyes ... speechless, he carried on by saying I looked back at you twice tonight to get your attention, do you know what I was trying to tell you? Still speechless, I shock my head no well, If you were actually paying attention these last few days you would have noticed all of this, but you were only focused on one thing and you missed the big picture. I wouldn't mind teaching you if you don't mind learning. I shock my head, but was able to speak this time and said hell yeah! I want to learn. He said ok, get some rest, we start in the morning.

CHAPTER 4

I was awakened early Thursday morning at 4:30 sharp. Mr. Johnson gave me fifteen minutes to dress, eat breakfast and meet him by the back door. We had a two mile jog to get to the dogs, feed and walk them then a two mile jog back where we showered and got ready for the rest of our day. I stepped back into my room to find a book on my bed, 48 Laws of Hustling. As he walked past my door he told me that I should read the book and let him know what I took from it, I finished getting dressed and we left out to head to the school. To the least of my knowledge my training had already begun to mold me into what I will later become. Friday morning had us follow the same routine, but Saturday was a little different. We started the day off at 4:30 as usual, but instead of us heading back after we fed and walked the dogs we headed south. At this point I was confused but learned early to just follow his lead. We power walked for a few miles until we happened upon a building that appeared to be abandoned. With a forceful knock the steel warehouse door slid up to reveal a full gym. He reached out to shake the women's hard that opened the door, slid in and motioned me to slide the door back down. This place was known as La cola del escorpion the scorpion's tail from the intense pain that your body endures while working out there. Mr. Johnson turned to me and explained that this is where I would spend my weekends until further notice, shook the lady's hand again then hurried off as if he was late to a meeting. The lady then turned to me with a hand gesture leading me in the direction that she wanted me to go while she introduced herself. My name is not important, but since we will be working out together you can simply call me La reina, (the queen). We'll get you started with this jump rope, let me see how many you can do without stopping. After three hours of push ups, sit ups, jump rope and burpees I was exhausted. That is it for the day, Mr. Johnson is home waiting for you to arrive.

After what seemed like a marathon, I finally made it back the house. Mr. Johnson was sitting in the living room when I walked in. He only nodded as I walked thru to get to my room. After a quick shower I was told to get some rest because we're doing it again tomorrow, but I think I was sleep before the whole sentence came out. 4:30 came entirely too quick, I was still exhausted from the day before, We did the exact same thing for three months straight until my body finally got used to this rigorous regiment. On the first Saturday of the fourth month, my training suddenly switched up. Instead of burpees and jump ropes. I was

The Hansom Hustla

introduced to stretch pants and yoga mats. This was welcomed change, and on top of all of that this gave my body the much needed time for recovery. With a clear mind and a not so broken down body, I got up the courage to ask Mr. Johnson about the items on the kitchen table. "If you don't mind me asking, what's up with all the stuff on the table? Are you that forgetful or are you just a collector or something. Mr. Johnson peered over the top of whatever book he was reading to say " finally", "I was wondering when you were going to ask", I followed him into the kitchen where I saw at least thirteen different wallets grouped together, but with a particular order to them, "I lifted all of these on our trips home. I grouped them together in chronological order", While pointing at the group of two, four and seven he proceeded to say, "these two are from the first Monday, these four are from that Tuesday and these seven are from the Wednesday that we took the long way back here. I turned to you to see if you had caught it when I did it, but your head was in the clouds". My jaw dropped, it took me back to the first day that we met and he told me that my technique was sloppy. He was so graceful and quick that I didn't see him even lift a finger. He continued to saying, Now that you've inquired about this, we can finally start your real training. The next few weeks were a little overwhelming, we exercised endlessly for the next month, Lack of sleep and soreness had me not knowing if I was coming or going.

My time with La reina intensified too. We went from exercising and yoga to her introducing me to boxing then wrestling and eventually judo. Judo was my favorite of the three especially when I learned that I could incorporate one of the things that I love with it. Since judo has a lot to do with pressure points & joints on the body. It took me back to what I learned about the human body in biology class. I trained like this for a year and a half when Mr. Johnson felt that it was time for a little break. So he took me fishing. With only a knife, a string and a hook we headed down to the river that was located deep in the woods. As we hiked through the woods Mr. Johnson would be giving me nature lessons like what plants or berries were safe to eat, how to find out the cardinal directions and what makes what sounds. Since I didn't get out much, this quickly became my favorite thing to do. This carried on throughout the summer and with the fall season vastly approaching we started increasing our time out. It went from being just a fishing trip to us actually camping out in the middle of nowhere. We changed locations every time we went out so that we wouldn't disturb the animal's natural habitats. This time it seemed like we were hiking for hours before he settled on a spot. We pitched a tent and set up the camp ground. It was getting late so we built a fire, as it blazed thoroughly and the orange-reddish color danced off the darkness around us, Mr. Johnson told me that he'd have to go get some more wood for the fire then scurried off in the night. After about thirty minutes I started to worry because he hadn't come

The Hansom Hustla

back yet and it seemed like the lower the fire get the louder the noises got that echoed the woods, I was terrified. In a panic I threw any-thing in the fire that would burn hoping that it would keep the animals away, and after about an hour of doing this I realized that I was alone in the woods by myself with no food, a small amount of water to drink and a dying fire. With a last desperation move I ran to the parts of the woods that was illuminated by the fire, took every stick I could find and some pine straw and threw it all in the fire then closed myself up in the tent to cry with the sounds of multiple paws crunching leaves outside the tent, I leaped out of sleep out of fear. They were so close to the tent that I could hear them panting then all of a sudden everything stopped, Then everything fell silent. I was curled up in the middle of this tent praying that what ever that was out there would simply go away. But it didn't! The grouped thuds of what seemed to be a herd was headed straight towards me them stopped right outside of the tent's door. The zipper slowly crept up to start to reveal the down of morning and within a split second, pharaoh, my favorite young pup rushed in the tent to greet me with kisses. Upon me climbing out of the tent, Bryant asked why I just didn't come home or at least keep the fire going last night? I explained to him how terrified I got after he left and that I pretty much forget everything that I was taught. (I hadn't felt like that since the day I lost my best friend Ebony so many years ago. Mr. Johnson left me alone, at that moment I felt like he left me there to die and I held a grudge in my heart for that). On our three-four hour hike to put up the dogs then home, I said nothing, I barely looked his way the whole time, We climbed the hill to his house and all I could think about was me being out there alone and how I was a fool for letting my guard down around this man. We entered the house and I headed straight to the bathroom to shower: The hot water seemed so therapeutic with every pulsating drop. I got out the shower to find another book on my bed entitled master your emotions, I guess he figured that it'll be better for me to read the book than actually talking things out. The next morning we were at it again at 4:30 sharp. We were doing variations of the same routine everyday with a different combat tactic thrown in every four to six months. In-between my training sessions Mr. Johnson would have me sharpen my "lifting" and "boosting" skills by going to all the high security stores & areas to "pick up" certain things. It was never as simple as lifting a wallet off of a shopper, it was a watch off of a certain dealer's wrist or a ring from some wealthy lady's finger. The items and victims became more detailed every time. Three and a half years had gone by before I was ever introduced to any sort of weapons. La reina was the one who started me with my weapons training. I was taught how to control and handle the bans staff. It was awkward at first until I learned that the balance of the staff is controlled by your body's movements and how flexible it is   , but stern & solid when it needs to be. I worked with this one the most. I loved the distance that I could strike from and found that it was quite the defensive weapon as

The Hansom Hustla

well. The straight sword is the second weapon that was taught to me by La reina, this was somewhat easier than the bang to learn how to control. We trained with these two weapons for at least six months until one Saturday towards the beginning of spring. I entered the gym to see four other people there besides La reina. From the time that I opened the door to La cola del escorpion until the time that I left that day, No one spoke, I stepped towards the center of the practice mat where I was blind sided by a kick to the ribs. As I turned to defend myself I was punched from the opposite side. This attack lasted for about an hour until La reina figured that I had enough. The other four people were dismissed and as La reina helped me up off the floor she asked what was I expecting to happen when I saw the unfamiliar faces? She also stated that you've been training here for years and she thought that I'd be more prepared for this, Go home, Mr. Johnson is waiting for you, As I walked into the house Mr. Johnson glanced up at me and said, we're switching your training tomorrow. The next day at 4:30 sharp we were up for our jog after out shower Mr. Johnson grabbed a bag motioned me to grab the other and we headed out the back door. We drove four-six hours for what I thought was another camping trip, unloaded the truck and proceeded to an opening in the tree line. To my surprise the break in the tree line revealed a completely set up outside range. This is where I learned to load, unload, point, aim & shoot damn near every caliber weapon. Mr. Johnson taught me everything, about a weapon, I learned about the different bullet grains, what the purpose of every type of bullet is how to maintain the weapon and the most important part, cleaning the weapon. For the next couple of years I went through these exercise with La reina and Mr. Johnson. Throughout the rest of my training I was introduced to two other combat weapons, the broadsword and the spear. These two years were the most intense. Every week or any random days it'll be four new people at the gym. After three weeks of fighting random groups of people I found that I had to strike first the only issue is to find out who to attack first. I spent my next two trips to the gym training to pen points a pattern of their attacks. Even though it was different people every time, I figured that it had to be some sort of attack pattern. The first time I was attacked it was from a kicks to the ribs, the second time it was a grappler ... this last time I was taken down by a leg sweep. If I'm not mistaken then the attack should be form someone who strikes to the head the next time. Either way it goes I believe that I'd be ready. I knew what to expect and between my training and a few books that I read on strategies like the Art of war and 100 deadly skills I should be more than prepared, but I never went back to the gym. Instead of the gym we took a 180 and went back to the city and back to Mr. Johnson's place. Where we went back to our previous routine. Our first night back we started back working. Even though I enjoyed our time off the grid I can truly say that I missed the steady noise of the traffic, the lights that lit up the night and bustle of the street traffic, as we stopped at the last light before

The Hansom Hustla

the left turn to climb the hill to Bryant's house. We quickly unpacked and headed back downtown. I could immediately tell that my training had definitely sharpened my skills, I was moving smoother and was noticeably faster with a lot more confidence. Doing this for the next two nights seemed more like a vacation than work.

A week before daylight savings time Mr. Johnson gave me the task of "picking up" us new winter clothes. Since I'd only experienced new clothes a few short years ago I was more than willing to go shopping to pick up us some new garments. I woke up anxious and excited Monday morning, we started the day with our normal routine, got home, showered then dressed. I was just about to head down the hallway to the back door when I was called back Mr. Johnson. He informed me that we would be taking one last camping trip at the end of the year so make sure that I get something warm enough for the trip. This was the first time that Mr. Johnson sent me out alone on a mission, but it wouldn't be my last. This was a big task so I was given a week to complete it. A few days and countless hours of lifting, boosting and sometimes actually buying items, I felt like I picked us up enough clothes to last us two winters. As I was leaving Friday morning to pick up the last couple of items on my list I got that weird feeling. You know the kind of feeling that makes the hairs on the back of your neck stand-up? Yeah, that feeling. I looked around just to find no one there, but this feeling is too uncomfortable and familiar that I couldn't ignore it, I walked back in the house to check if Mr. Johnson was still there because the last time that I got this eerie feeling he was the one that was following me. I couldn't explain or think of why I would have this feeling because Mr. Johnson was still planted sternly in his oversized recliner reading a book. I eventually just shock it off and chalked it up as being something that was just in my head, and proceeded on to do the rest of my shopping. Boots, gloves, beanies and coats were the last items on my list and for these items I headed to one of my favorite stores, Saks.

Heading back to the house I noticed an odd color SUV sitting in a handicap space close to the mall entrance. Besides the odd color, the out of state license plate drew my attention. Thinking how odd it was to see Mexico plates in this city especially right before winter. I admired the vehicle in passing as I hurried down the street towards the subway. Eight stops later I exited the train head down the stairs then up another flight to get out to the street, went down a block and stopped by the subway at the bottom of the hill that sat on the corner for lunch. Upon entering the restaurant I caught a glimpse of a homeless man begging for change in the window which shouldn't have stuck out to me, but we have the lowest homeless rate in the U.S. according to the latest statistics and they're even more rare in this part of town. I grabbed my order and proceeded up the hill to the house when all of a sudden, I got that eerie feeling again. Thinking to myself that this is third time today, this can't be a coincidence, someone has to be following me. I sped up

The Hansom Hustla

slightly to go ahead and get in the house so that I can tell Mr. Johnson that I believe that I was being followed. I burst through the door and blurted out his name, my voice just echoed through the house without any response. I checked the living room, then kitchen, I ran downstairs to check the back door, then back up to my room, Mr. Johnson was nowhere to be found. I headed down the ball to Bryant's bedroom, slowly turned the knob and just as I was pushing the door open I heard a loud boom then the whole house went black instantly. I immediately got low after I heard what sounded like the window to the front door break. I was frozen in the hallway but calm surprisingly. I heard two sets of footsteps suddenly fill the silence, one set headed downstairs towards the back of the house while the other set headed towards me and the bedrooms. The person crept down the hall carefully easing down the hall pausing after each step to try to maintain their stealthiness. I stayed low to make sure that I would stay undetected ... my heart started to race faster and faster with their every step until they were close enough for me to strike. I wanted to be as quiet as possible so I wouldn't alert the person downstairs so I choose an uppercut to lift their head up just enough for me to slip behind them and apply a rear naked choke, they were out in a ????. I snuck back down the hallway towards the kitchen, grabbed the baseball bat that Mr. Johnson kept behind his chair at the table and hid at the top of the stairs. I could hear the other person lightly rambling around downstairs, after about fifteen minutes of rambling they started back up the stairs. As they reached the top of the stairs I swung & took their knees out with a loud scream the lights popped back on.

CHAPTER 5

Stop this nonsense immediately! Mr. Johnson shouted. As I stood over the home invader that was laying on the ground holding his knee. Looking at me holding the bat to the corrupt, Mr. Johnson fixed his eyes on the hurt man to ask if his leg was broken, gave me that look that I had grown to kinda fear while he pushed pass me. He walked to the kitchen to grab a chair then helped the man up into the chair. After a brief analysis of the dude's leg Mr. Johnson began to banage up the dude's left leg right below the knee. Leaving on the wall in the hallway I couldn't help but to notice that the dude looked like an older version of Bryant. Partially through him getting banaged up the older man asked Mr. Johnson, "Where's Lenny", with a confused look on his face, Mr. Johnson responded by asking "Lenny is here?" while glancing over his shoulder in my direction. Seeing that was my que to talk I chimed in with "you must be speaking about the other dude that's passed out in the hallway". After two more circles with the wrap around the older dude's leg, Mr. Johnson hurried down the hall to tend to the other victim. A few slaps to the face and some smelling salt quickly revived the Lenny dude. Bryant helped him back down the hallway to the kitchen and sat him next to the older gentleman. With a closer look, I couldn't help but to think to myself that I knew this dude from somewhere I just couldn't figure where. Ten more minutes of the three men chatting with each other revealed that the two trespassers were related to Mr. Johnson. The one I hit in the leg, Glen, was a few years older and henny, the younger brother tends to stop by every once in awhile to check up on Bryant. They let themselves in with the spare key that Bryant leaves above the door frame and the loud boom that I heard just before they entered was the sound of a circuit breaker exploding, they split up in the house to search for the circuit box. Bryant had been outside in the back trying to get the generator to crank up when he heard Glen scream in pain.

    With one last tug of the generator cord it finally rumbled to life as Bryant span around heading back to the house all in one motion. After assessing the situation, getting everyone calmed down and injuries seen about, Bryant looked towards Lenny and asked if it was close to being that time again? Lenny just gave him a look that jarred my memory of where I saw him before, he was the homeless man that I noticed across from subway earlier that day. The glance said everything that Bryant needed to know without saying anything at all. Mr. Johnson slowly stood up and started walking towards his room when the silence was broken

The Hansom Hustla

by Glen's phone. He let it ring twice then answered with a simple "yes" there was no words spoken on his side of the call just a few head nods, as if the other person could see him, then ended the call with "I understand the three men glared at each other, but no words were spoken. I was confused by the whole series of events. Even though I was all caught up on the three of them being related, I had no clue what else just went on. Glen was the first to actually speak by saying "they'll be sending the information to my phone shortly" and "I won't be able to make this one because of obvious reasons". Lenny chimed in by saying "we seem to be a man short" and peered in my direction. "She seems to be ready to me" Bryant replied with "she'll have to be" then turned in my direction and said firmly "pack of bag for a week", "pack lite, but warm". Without hesitation nor question asked I swiftly turned and rushed to my room to do what I was told. Thinking to myself that I know that this can't be a causal trip so I picked all dark colors, hopefully it will be within Mr. Johnson's approval. Six minutes later I was back by the entrance of the kitchen packed and ready to go with no idea of what these three brothers had signed me up for. Fifteen minutes after Glen hung up his phone a single beep got everyone's attention, especially mine since I was the only one out of us four that had no clue as to what is going on. Glen read the contents of the message and stated that Jim will be at the location in thirty minutes and we needed to leave now if we plan on catching that ride. Mr. Johnson, Lenny and I hurried to Glen's SUV parked outside while Glen informed Mr. Johnson that he'll forward the rest of the information to his phone.

It was a short ride to what seemed to be an abandoned air strip, but seemed endless. Where shortly after a helicopter appeared out of nowhere, landed and a tall wiry dude submerged from the cab and through all of the dust and smoke. The three men all greeted each other with a slight smile and bro hug then the tall guy fixed his eyes on me, straightened his face and nodded my way as to say, who is she? Mr. Johnson replied by saying "she's with me, one is down so I brought her along". The tall man, who I found out later that his name is actually Jim, but goes by Hawk, asked is she ready for this? Mr. Johnson stated that I'll have to be as we locked and boarded the Hello. When we tool off my throat dropped to my stomach and my stomach to my butt as we zoomed below radar at seemingly break neck speed. I was pinned to my chair, mostly due to me being scared out of my mind and from the maneuvering that Hawk left necessary to get us to our destination. Upon arrival in Czechia we were left with our luggage, an equipment bag and a "see you in four days" from Hawk. We hiked for around five to six miles until we settled in a small cottage that was at least another eight miles from the city, started a fire and unpacked. This is where I was finally filled in on what was going on and why we were here. Over our dinner I was told that we were called here on a mission to locate and extract a child that was taken from their mother by a man simply known as Velký Medvěd or the big bear. He's known by this

The Hansom Hustla

name because of the bear skin that he wears all the time. Rumors say that he wears the skin as a trophy from surviving the brown bear attack in which he so-called killed the bear but was left with a visible claw mark that claimed his right eye. He was last known to have taken a little boy as his own from the child's mother that refused to bare a child for him. He's been sighted back here in his home country where he feels he's most protected. Since Glen wasn't here to do it, it was my job to make the eight mile hike alone to the village and see if I could spot Velký Medvěd, report back to Mr. Johnson and Lenny who's job was to extract the child by any means necessary. We had a total of three more days to fulfill the mission and get back to the pick up point before the end of the fourth day. If we weren't there on day four, Hawk's instructions were to leave us dead or alive and report back to whomever sent us on this mission in the first place. The next morning I set off on my journey to the village and all I could think about was I guess this is the reason he head me training for so long. I smiled to myself thinking and all this time I thought that I was training to become a better pick-pocketer. After roughly a 5 hour hike I arrived at the village. At first glance it seemed to be a fairly poor town with street merchants and entertainers that lined the street looking to make a fast buck, but no more than an hour of me being there I was approached by two armed men that were angrily gelling at me. I finally figured out that they were private guards and was not so nicely telling me to come with them and since I didn't speak the language, and they had to repeat themselves more than twice, they found it disrespectful and I was to be taken back to the main quarters to be taught a lesson. Once at the main quarters I kept my eyes open to see if I could catch a glimpse of anything or anyone that might look familiar. I was instructed to merely just push a button on the inside of my collar whenever I recognize anyone which will alert Lenny and Mr. Johnson of my location and they would take care of the rest. I was led to a small room that paralleled what seemed to be some sort of dining area. I was found to give up my jacket, where the button to contact Mr. Johnson was, and my boots. Barefoot and cold, I had no idea what to expect. My thoughts were racing as to how I could get out of this situation. Unknowing of where I was inside this house more exactly where I was in this foreign country, it had me thinking about to the first weeks of my training when Bryant left me in the woods to fend for myself, but I was better now and more focused. I wasn't the same little girl that was terrified to come out of the tent them all of a sudden the tiniest voice came from around the corner that broke my inner thoughts asking in a heavy Czech accent, "who are you and why are you in my country?" I guess the guards knew who the tiny voice belonged to as they snapped to attention when they heard it. "I've checked your garments and haven't found anything, not even an i.d.". "So I ask you again, as the person attached to the voice submerged from the shadows, who are you?" I recognized the man that bore the claw scar immediately, it was big bear with the young boy and three more guards

The Hansom Hustla

at tow. I said nothing, only looked in somewhat humor because this man known as Velký Medvěd couldn't have been no larger than I was in height and even though he was in pretty good physical shape, his arms were too short to box off a fly. As he rushed up to me as if to intimidate me, he asked me again "why are you in my country?!!" I didn't speak word, but his malodorous breath had me covering my nose. Big bear took this as the ultimate disrespect and summoned all the guards to teach me a lesson as he and the child slowly retracted back into the shadows. All I know was that I had an opportunity to rescue this child and couldn't lose it. Following the two down the hall as far as I could hear them, I was struck from behind from the first guard which stumbled me forward a couple to steps. The next strike was a swift kick to the legs. All of this seemed way too familiar from the time that I spent at La cola del escorpion with La reina and I knew now exactly how to defend myself from these attacks. I met the next punch with a punch of my own then a swift knee to the groin which doubled him over then a sharp jab to the nose then turned to the second guard who was charging me, stopped him in his tracks with a straight kick to the knee that was sure to break his kneecap as he lied there holding his knee screaming in pain I snatch the pendant from his jacket and thrusted it in his ear, killing him before his head hit the ground. Looking up in time to see the third guard fumbling with his hand gun searching for the safety, but could never get a hold of the gun completely before he was struck with a kick to the ear. This gave me an opening to get out of the small room. I ran across the narrow hallway to the dining area with the fourth and fifth guards on my heels. I managed to grab a hold of a knife that I threw as I span towards them, the guard right behind me was able to dodge it but caught the fifth one in the shoulder. I stopped running at a long sturdy dinner table, this is the place the fourth guard thought he had me cornered. As he charged me I was able to side step and hit him with an elbow to the back of the head that slammed his face into the solid oak with a thud and was able to finish the last one with a sterling silver dinner tray as soon as he was able to jar the knife out of his shoulder.

Heavily breathing, possibly due to a broken rib, I was able to find my jacket and boots tossed in the hallway while following it in the direction that I heard big bear's footsteps go earlier. The hallway led me to another which led me to a flight of swirling steps. I rested at the top of the stairs just long enough to get my boots back on. Not even sure if I was headed in the right direction I started down the steps. As I got at least halfway down the steps when I noticed a dancing of a fire that warmed me even though I was on the steps and had no idea where it was located. I stopped there to study the shadows that slowly moved about in the illumination of the dancing fire's light. I could make out what seemed to be the tiny man and the little boy, but it was something or someone else clown there that I couldn't quite make out. While standing there motionless, my ears where greeted by another set of footsteps coming towards me. I had to react

The Hansom Hustla

fast, but what do I do? The steps came closer and closer down the hallway and now at the stairs, my mind was racing and so was my heart. Four more steps and whomever it was would be right here looking at me face to face, three more, then two.... I had no choice but to rush the person to try and get the upper hand. I took off towards the person catching him by surprise, before he could let out a word I punched him in the throat, kneed him in the private and an upper cut with my elbow to his face that knocked him out cold. As I stood over this unconscious man I noticed that this was the guard from earlier that I kicked in the head. Remembering that this was the same dude that was fumbling the handle of his gun. I quickly searched and found his piece and came up with a plan. Dragging his body down a few more steps then rolled him to bottom of the steps just to find out what it was that I couldn't make out from the glare of the fire. With a deepened roar and a swipe of a paw I realized that it was a fully grown bear chained to a wall by his foot. The guard's body fell just out of the reach of the bear's claw, but must've startled him because of it sprung onto it's feet as the guard hit the floor. I was maybe a step or two behind the guard when I came down the steps with pistol in hand aimed right for Velký Medvěd. I motioned him to step away from the child with the barrel of the gum and gentle told the child to come to me. Velký Medvěd side stepping stated "Oh, so you do speak" while stepping away be slowly removed the bear far from around his neck and shoulders to reveal his stubby arms and wide chest he stated that I'll never make it out of the house alive. Then as soon as I looked down to grab the young boy's hand he rushed me, I stepped in front of the child to protect him and squeezed the trigger of the gun. There was a click, but nothing, I squeezed the trigger two 10 more times, click, click, still nothing. This durn guard was walking around with a gun without bullets! After the third click big bear was right in front of me and scooped me up in a beer hug that made me scream in pain from my already broken rib. His short arms squeezed tighter and tighter which made me drop the empty gun. With all of the strength that I could master up I kneed him in the leg, it did nothing. I could feel the heat of his breath on my neck beckoning me to give up then out of nowhere a sound of a thud across the back of his head made him loosen his grip as he reached up to feel the warm blood roll down the back of his head to his neck, dropping me in the process, as he slowly turned around his eyes locked with the little boy who stood there with a fire poker gripped firmly in both hands and stumbled backwards tripping over the guard that was still laid out at the bottom of the stairs falling just inside the reach of his "pet" bear who didn't waste any time biting and clawing at the wound in his head. I jumped up immediately grabbing the young boy's hard and fled up the steps. We could still hear Velký Medvěd's cries as we hurried down the hallway as the real big bear tore him apart.

    The sun was rising on our fourth day and we had a lot of ground to cover to get back to Lenny & Mr. Johnson and even further to go to catch our ride. After a few wrong turns

The Hansom Hustla

in the house that made us back track we finally found an exit that led us nowhere, we were in the middle of the back of the house that come to find out, was built as a circle. We had to reenter the house through the rear, locate the main floor then find the main entrance. What seemed to be an hour later we finally found the main entrance and whisked away as quickly as possible to the small village, we started our eight mile journey back to the cottage to meet back up with Lenny and Mr. Johnson. About a mile and a half into it the little boy began dragging the pace, we will never make it in time if we continue at this pace and as far as we have to go he's bound to walk slower so I picked him up and also the pace. Cold and injured I really wasn't doing any better, but I was determined to get us there. About four or maybe five miles in I started hearing a buzzing sound that was vastly approaching. I stopped to put little man down so that I could retrieve two filleting knives that I managed to pick up while roaming through the house. The buzzing got amplified as it got closer, I stood my ground ready for whatever of whomever it may be. In the not so far distance I could make out two men, one on a dirt bike the other on a four wheeler as they zoomed closer I heard a familiar voice yelling "Do you know how long we've been looking for you?!" then another familiar voice saying "Get on! We only have a few hours to catch our ride". It was the voices of Lenny & Mr. Johnson, I dropped the knives in relief. Hurrying to the pick up point Bryant could see that I was physically hurt but we had no time to stop to nurse my injuries upon arrival at the pick up point we grabbed our bags and threw them aboard as Hawk fired up the engine while yelling "you all were cutting it close this time" with henny yelling back "Someone wanted to be a renegade their first time out and go at it alone". The brief conversation lasted a minute or two longer as I drifted off from exhaustion. We seemed to have arrived at the air strip as swiftly as we left, unload everything and all the men said their goodbyes as Hawk got to me he extended his hand and said "Great work, hopefully we'll be working together again soon" turned and jumped back into the ??? and was gone as soon as he came.

Glen's SUV was still parked in the abandoned hanger where we left it, we loaded up and headed back to the house. No sooner than we stepped in the house Glen's phone rung, he picked up after the second ring and simply said "yes" nodded a few times just as before and hung up right after saying "I understand", It had already been arranged that Henny & Glen would take the boy to his mother first thing in the morning. Glen was waiting for the details to come through when his phone rung again, looking puzzled he answers it again after the second ring with a "yes", spun around towards my direction and extended his phone to me all while saying "It's for you".

CHAPTER 6

It was a warm, beautiful spring afternoon, The birds were chirping and the children were playing without a care in the world. One would say it was a perfect day, perfect for everyone but me and Daniel Stanley that is. I was nervous as hell but calm, and Daniel never saw me coming. I will never forget that day because despite of all of my training, I still didn't believe that I was ready. On May 16th 2002, I became a killer. Everything that I'd done prior to this day was either for training or self-defense, but today... yeah today was different, on this day killing became my job.

Daniel was my first so I'll always remember him, him and several more after him. It took me a few years to learn how to suppress the memories, but I still can't get my first six victims out of my head. Every one of them had an unique story that led to the faculty calling my phone. Daniel, for example, ran an underground children's kidnapping ring that was responsible for the disappearance of over eight hundred children from all over the world. These kids were made to do all types of things from working in sweat shops to being involved in sex crimes. I was given the assignment to take him out by any means necessary with a week's time frame to do so. I studied Daniel's every move for six days (day & night), chose my weapon and made my move. He always seemed to be heavily guarded usually five to six men that were always in plain clothes in order to blend in with the crowd and only traveled in bullet proof cars, so I figured that the only way that I would be able to complete my mission would either be a long distance shot that would probably cause a scene or get up close and personal. I choose to get up close that way I could just float through the crowd, which I did. My love for marine life played a part in my weapon's decision. In my studies I found that the blue-ringed octopus, even though very small, packed enough venom to kill up to 26 adult humans within about a thirty minute window and with no known antidote, I figured this would be perfect for my line of work.

By night four I had found a way to extract the venom and prepared my weapon. I decided to use a thumbtack, as weird as that might sound, but it was small enough to not be seen and would penetrate enough skin to get into the victim's blood stream. I was able to simply brush pass him, tap him on the shoulder with a polite "excuse me" and head straight to my vehicle a block away. Thirty-five minutes later my phone rung with a voice on the other end stating "you did a good thing today, we'll be contacting you again as needed". I couldn't tell you how many times my

The Hansom Hustla

phone rung after that particular day, but I can tell you that with me using this method that I've had an one hundred percent kill rate over my long career.

    Two months later my phone rang and I was informed that my next victim would be simply known as "Bull". Bull was an arms dealer that only dealt with the lower class criminals in third world countries. Drug cartels and malicious groups were his number one clients. During my research I found that Bull's real name was Clint, Clint Cartmoore and was actually the father of the confident girl in Mr. Johnson's class, Cindy, and even though her education was paid in full to any institution that she'd like, she chose to go to a Ju-co to prove to her family that she could make her own way in which ever venture she chose. I couldn't lie and say that I didn't feel some type of way about this hit because even though Cindy and I didn't actually see eye to eye on our individual views, I still felt that I had a personal tie to Bull. I had to figure out a way to not feel guilty about killing him. During my first days of observation he seemed like a typical family man. He dropped what I believed were Cindy's two younger siblings off at school by 7:15 every morning and was back in the parking lot before the three O'clock bell rung everyday. He seemed to handle his business affairs outside of the house in a studio that he had across town, which led me to believe that his wife had no idea what he really did for a living. He sat and ate dinner with the family every night and would always be in eye sight of a television to make sure that he was able to catch sport center's top ten plays. It wasn't until he started drinking that I could see why Cindy chose a small school three states away. Bull would turn extremely violent while downing at least a fifth of rum before one in the afternoon and another that he consumed for dinner. As he yelled and knocked over lamps, chairs, TVs and anything else that he would claim to be in his way. He had slap his wife around then proceed to rape her passing out from being too drunk just as soon as he started. This enraged me and by day five I couldn't take anymore and sprung into action. Because of how badly he beat his wife she wouldn't be able to cook dinner at times so they often ordered out from an online restaurant called Kira's touch, it was a fairly new spot that was ran by an always buoyant young lady by the name of Kira. This place offered everything from pizzas to pastries. I spotted my chance as soon as I saw the delivery car entering the neighborhood, flagged the delivery driver down and gave him a bogus story about being Bull's eldest daughter that snuck back intown from school to surprise the family, gave him a twenty dollar tip and proceeded on to the house to deliver the food. Before I could even get out of the car clint swung the front door open yelling profanities towards my way. I exited the car with the family dinner in tow, apologized about the tardiness and handed him two bags containing three boxes a piece with a two liter soda. Gave him a quick prick on the finger as he snatched the food from my hands then turned and walled away then he slammed the door in my face… He was the only victim that I visually saw die. From my surveillance spot on top of

The Hansom Hustla

the hill within the tree line, I could see him plop down in his favorite chair and turn on sports center... he was dead before top ten got to the number four slot. It was around that same time I got word that Bull had also provided guns to Daniel's operation and, his personal men to ??? Daniel for his protection.

I drove away from the Cartmoore's neighborhood feeling like I did the family a favor. From what I'd learned Wendy, Bull's wife didn't call the police until at least a day later. "The faculty put me right back to work a week later giving me a target that I'd seen a few times before. A lady this time that I use to always see making statements on the news. Veronica was the only name that I received during the phone call then a picture shortly after. It was definitely the lady that would make all the news statements about every big bust that was made in Oklahoma City in the last three years. Her name was Veronica, Veronica Zaccari. Veronica was an eager cop when she first got out of the academy. She wanted to learn the most she could and clean the streets of the drugs and violence that seemed to go hand and hand throughout the city. Zaccai's first partner was a by-the-books vet by the name of Jabour that taught her how to move, what to look for and most importantly, how to get back home safely to her family every night. Jabour had three years left to be eligible for early retirement when Zaccari joined the force. After Jabour's retirement Veronica refused to work with anyone else and made a name for herself as a take no junk type of cop who wasn't afraid to get physical with you if need be. Her arrests always stuck and her numbers stayed consistent every year. It wasn't until she made detective that some questions started arising about the way she did her job, but that didn't stop her from becoming the city's first woman and youngest Deputy chief. From the outside looking in Zaccari was the pillar of the police force. It wasn't long until I found out how she managed to be in the right place at the right time every time something big happened in the city. Come to find out that she was working with Daniel. Daniel would cut her in on the profits of his operation in trade for her raid tips and certain children's and what underground criminals were making noise whereabouts she would also withhold vital information that might lead to a child being found so that Daniel could get in and out of town undetected. Learning all of this information made it easy for me to think of a plan. I felt that it wouldn't be too smart to actually meet her in her office so I sent word that I needed to speak with her immediately about my son that had been missing for a week now. I led her to believe that it was a high profile kidnapping and that I couldn't run the risk of being seen entering nor leaving the police precinct for fear of someone spotting me and doing harm to my child. She agreed to meet me later that evening in a small local bar outside of Oklahoma City in Shawnee. I arrived at nine then Veronica shortly after around nine twenty, we talked at a table in the far corner of the room for about fifteen to twenty minutes convincing her to take a good look into my missing son's disappearance. We got up to exit the building

The Hansom Hustla

and as I turned to thank her so very much, I reached out my right hand to shake hers and as I covered both our hands with my left, I ever so gently pricked her with the stick pen that hung from my jacket sleeve. I apologized by saying that it was a new coat that I received from my child during Christmas and I must've not gotten all the pens out before I slipped it on. By six a.m her death was all over the news. The newscaster spoke "on breaking news this morning the deputy chief, Veronica Zaccari, was found dead in the garage of her high rise apartment building this morning." "Reports say that she drove into the garage around ten forty-five last night, but never made it out of her vehicle". "She didn't have anything that appeared to be missing from her car or person so the police are ruling out this being a robbery gone bad", "More about this tragic death later in our broadcast".... I actually got a bonus for that one, as soon as the death of veronica aired my phone rung again, this time for a job in the skirts of Atlanta. Actually a pretty decent ride east of Atlanta in a city called Conyers. I was looking for another one of Daniel's associates that was only known by his nickname, Man Man. I was told that he went into hiding shortly after Daniel's death and fled the state when he got word that Veronica was murdered thinking that it would only be a short time before whoever this person and or person's was would be after him next due to his connection to Daniel & Veronica. Man Man was smart, only moving under the blanket of the night. It actually took me a little longer and all of my GA. resources to locate him. A week and a half of searching led me to the city of Conyers where I was led to believe that he took refuge with family and friends, Man Man was Daniel's right hand man. His job was to lure innocent kids away from their homes or schools in order to get snatched and drugged by Daniel himself. This would seem to be a fairly easy task because Man Man looked and dressed exactly like a teenager himself, he could blend in at any and every school function or hangout around the city. I never actually laid eyes on Man Man, just pictures. He seemed to always be one step ahead of me one way or another. I would draw a blank when it came down to how I would be able to get to Man Man since I had no real pattern to go off of. Two weeks into it and the faculty was losing faith in me and threatened to give my assignment to someone else, that's when I finally got a break. While surveying what I found out was his mother's house, I caught her coming out of the house tripping over a freshly delivered box from FedEx. I overheard her yelling at him to come get this durn box from in-front of her door and that's when I got the idea... his online shopping will truly be the death of him. I noticed that almost every Tuesday there would be at least three boxed delivered to his mothers address. All I would have to do is go to the post office and get a brown box, wait for the packages to be delivered, grab one then strategically place my stick pen inside a pocket of an outfit or the insole of a shoe. I'd rebox the item inside the brown box that I picked up from the post office with a label that I printed at Kinko's then replace the box on the doorstep. Tuesday

The Hansom Hustla

came around and just like clock work it was a FedEx delivery, as soon as they left I spring into action. The box that I picked up was addressed to him and just happened to be a nice pair of sneakers. I ripped the insole out carefully placed the needle in and swiftly stuffed the insole back, stuffed the shoes in my ready-made box and sat it back at the door as if nothing had happened. I couldn't tell who grabbed the packages off the porch, but what I did know is that after Man Man tried on those sneakers that that would be his last step. Two hours later I saw the ambulance rush to his mother's address. They spent around five minutes in the house then carted him out with the exact same shoes that I'd tampered with still on his feet.

It was somewhere between nine months and a year before I was contacted by the faculty again. They had made arrangements for Hawk to take me to the United Kingdom. with only knowing that I would get my instructions when I arrived. Two days and a seventeen hour flight later, my phone rang. I was informed this time about a couple, Mr. & Mrs. MacQuoid. The MacQuoid's had been moving around a lot from Belize to Brazil to the U.S. , Spain and even Thailand and now here in London. It was difficult at first to gather information on these two due to the constant traveling from country to country, but from what I could learn these two would travel around the globe taking in sights and also adopting a random child or two along the way. At first I really didn't see anything wrong with it especially because my reports listed Mrs. MacQuoid as having an ovarian condition that caused her not to be able to have kicks of her own. This was sad news and my heart hurt for her, for them as I took a deep sigh. But what more could a foster child want than to finally have a home with a mother and father that would raise them as their own? It would be an added bonus to have them be well off enough to take you around the world and learn of different cultures, customs and languages. I could only sit back and daydream about a fantasy life as such. A call from Mr. Johnson snapped me out of my trance, I couldn't get the fantasy I wanted but got more than just a father figure when I met him. I got stability, discipline, guidance, focus, responsibility and most importantly a friend. I answered my phone quickly with a mellow "Hello", he was short and to the point like he usually is, "Did you check your emails today?" He asked with a concerning voice. "No, Not Yet" was my response. He informed me that I might want to take a look at them then hung up, We made a rule a long time ago that we never discuss details over the phone, it will either be sent to a secured email or relayed in person. As I typed in my password to my email I figured that it would be some basic information on the McQuoid's that I could use in order for me to create a pattern so I can know where to strike, but this was some information that I wasn't ready for. According to these documents that I was starting at on my phone, this couple is the same couple that adopted Erica, my one and only true friend from so long ago. I was ecstatic at the thought that I could see my good friend again. So many thoughts rushed through my mind like, I

The Hansom Hustla

wonder if she still looks the same? How did life treat her after the orphanage? Is she still out spoken? And mainly if she simply even remembers who I am? I was frozen from the sudden thought of possibly being reunited with someone I lost so long ago. I was anxious to finally see her again, to ask her all about the exotic places that she'd probably been and the beautiful scenery she'd must've taken in. I couldn't wait any longer, I had to reach out to the MacQuoids to ask about her where abouts. The next morning would be the day that I would approach them to inquiry about my long lost friend. I wake up early Tuesday showered, dressed then checked the time on my phone, 7.19, still early the MacQuiods usually don't arrive to Monmouth until around 9. Since I had time to spare I went through my emails while catching the news. I had no clue what the news was actually saying since I don't speak a lick of French, but a face did catch my attention, it was Mrs. MacQuoid standing in the background of what seemed to be a story about a house fire, but the man she held so closely to her side wasn't Mr. MacQuoid. I rushed out of the hotel room to make sure that I'd arrive before Mr. & Mrs. MacQuoid. I needed to see exactly how they would arrive. I chose an outside seat that covered every angle and at 9 O'clock sharp Mr. MacQuoid came from the corner of Mercer St. and Mrs. MacQuoid from Shaftesbury Ave. to greet each other for what seemed like the first time today. I was curious to see what they would do, but never got too close. After what seemed to be around a twenty minute conversation they both departed the coffee shop in the same directions that they came. I decided to follow Mrs. MacQuoid thinking that she would be less likely to notice me trailing her. After more than a few turns and crossing a bridge, she stopped at Sir John Soane's museum. It was there when she caught up with the guy that I saw her with on the news. They greeted each other with a tight hug and proceeded to tour the museum. I couldn't lie and say that I wasn't taken back by a few of the exhibits myself, but my main focus was on Mrs. Quoid and the answers to my questions. After a long day of sight-seeing the two finally headed towards a loft north of the museum. I didn't want the man to be able to identify me so I laid low until the next day. 9 O'clock Wednesday morning couldn't come fast enough, I was at the coffee shop extra early anticipating the MacQuoid's arrival, something was different, they both had a concerning look on their faces. I sat close to ease drop on the conversation. Mr. MacQuoid was leaved over the table saying something about tomorrow will be the last time as Mrs. Quoid shook her head in agreeance. I decided to approach their table, "Excuse me, are you guys American?" They both looked up with Mr. Quoid having a look on his face as if I was bothering them. "Yes we are" spoke Mrs. Quoid, "I don't mean to bother you guys, but I'm having the hardest time finding my way around and an even harder time communicating." "Can you point me in the direction of the nearest orphanage?" Mr. MacQuoid's eyes got big while he instructed me to pull up a chair, as I sat down in-between the couple I could feel a barrel of a

The Hansom Hustla

gun poking me in my ribs. He demanded to know who I was and why I asked them of all people that particular question. I responded by simply saying that when I travel I like to visit the children because I can relate to growing up like they are, with him glaring at Me to figure out if he believed me or not, he finally eased up and took the gun out of my rib, told me what direction I should travel and sent me about my way. As I pushed back from the table I clumsily spilled his coffee all over him and the table. Mr. Quoid suddenly pushed back to avoid it getting more coffee on his clothes, I grabbed my napkin to help clean up the mess, dabbed his pants leg in order to surreptitiously prick him and then head about my way. I got halfway up the street when Mrs. MacQuoid called out to me. I guess she felt guilty about her role in what they had been doing so she opened up to me about how Mr. MacQuoid wasn't really her husband, they posed as a couple in order to adopt kids from certain orphanages. At the time Mr. MacQuoid and a man by the name of Daniel kept her drugged up off bufotenine toad venom. She had no idea what harm she was doing until she sobered up years later. She stated that she still meets up with Rainier because of the money that he owed her and because some organization threatened to kill both of them if they didn't keep going. She also stated that they hadn't had an assignment in durn near a year now, but she was still terrified especially with them learning that a few of the major players were recently killed. I figured from all the information she just told me that there was no way she'd remember my precious

Erica, but I had to ask. She told me the name didn't ring a bell, but the next thing she told me threw me all the way off.

The next morning my phone rang waking me from my slumber. The voice on the other end stated "You're getting sloppy, you actually let one get away". I just listened, "Nothing to say for yourself, hug?" "well, sit tight for your next assignment" then a click. The faculty might've had a different job for me, but I had my own objective now.

CHAPTER 7

My phone had to have rung twenty to thirty times since my trip to London. Sending me all over the world. From the extreme colds of Canada to the sandy beached of the Dominican Republic. If not for my line of work I would have to brag about my exploits, but I only went to these places for work purposes. I've only traveled with Mr. Johnson and rarely his brothers, Hawk has been my only means of transportation besides vehicles that were provided for us in various locations. Mostly I traveled alone to blend in better with the crowds and never took any form of public transportation to avoid anyone from being able to identify me. I've basically lived in the shadows for a these years, gathering intel on my victims, but never forgetting my personal objectives. Even though I still took my orders from the faculty, I was no longer a robot. My studies brought me closer to my prime target although I wasn't physically near them. Based off of the information that I was told by Mrs. MacQuoid, excuse me Gabby Wringger, I had to be close.

PRICK

My phone rung again, this time to come back to the states. The call landed me in a place that I was very familiar with. One could actually call this my home because this was the place I started my career. Although I was happy to be here, this time around felt like a distraction, but I was sent to do a job and like always, I'm going to make sure it gets done. My mission started off exactly like all of the others started before, I got a phone call with info and a picture would come after. I located my victim, studied them for around a week then I would strike. Even though this was my normal way of me conducting my business, this job was odd. Everything was too easy! My victim did exactly the same thing at the same times everyday. They would get up at six thirty every morning, shower, dress then off to work. They left work promptly at four p.m., stopped at the market to pick up their dinner then back home. This was the same routine each day for the five days that I studied them. I decided to strike on the last day of the weekend just before their bedtime. Entering Sunday evening I cautiously started to make my move, I rarely entered a victims place of residence but I figured that this would be the place that I would be less likely to be seen. I made my way towards the building of their apartment, but the closer I got to the breeze way the more of a creepy feeling that I got, like someone was watching my every move. Entering the building I walked to the far end of the building to the elevators across from the stairwell, pressed the up button on the elevator then waited patiently for the elevator to arrive. Upon arrival I quickly pressed the button for the seventh floor then darted to the staircase gently closing the door behind me in order to not be detected. Shortly after the elevator doors closed I heard footsteps vastly approaching the elevators. A tall slender figure appeared, checked to see what floor my elevator stopped on then turned towards the stairs. I was able to rush down a flight just before they entered the stairwell then head back towards the breeze way as they were on their way up. I was able to scurry through the building to the other set of elevators after sending the second one on this side up to the seventh as well. Headed up the other flight of stairs, in order to sneak up behind whomever went up the stairs to follow me, and lurk in the shadows. When I finally arrived to the seventh floor and headed down the hallway towards the first set of elevators I started to hear footsteps, the same footstep I heard in the breeze way. I slowly crept towards them as they seemed to be heading in my directions as well. I stopped and put my back on the wall while listening for the footsteps, they were so close now that I could hear the person breathing then all of a sudden, silence! Everything had just stopped, just as I was about to peak out a ding of the elevator cut through the quiet. Then the footsteps trailed off towards the elevators. I began pursuit but making sure I stayed in the few shadows that the hallway offered. The footsteps slowed when the person noticed that it was just the lady in seven sixteen coming back from walking her dogs. The small dogs barking distracted the person enough for me to close the gap between us without being heard. I still couldn't see the person's face because of the hoodie and mask they wore. I asked "why are you following me?" which startled the person, but not enough to stop them from turning around and throwing a backhanded punch simultaneously. The punch caught me off guard, but I quickly regained my composure right before the second punch was thrown. We tussled through the hallway with both of us struggling to get an advantage. After me landing a kick to the person's mid-section they were able to pull out a knife. Slicing at me furiously, they were able to cut me on my forearm, the pain made me curse, I had to get that knife out of their hand. They charged me, but with my smaller frame I was able to slightly side step them and catch them with a vicious blow near the ear and sweep their leg at the same time which made them trip and fall on the knife. The blade cut wide and deep which had to puncture a lung. They managed to roll over and pull down their mask the female uttered out "well played Mousy" right before choking to death on her own blood. I took a step back in shock just before I ran out of the building in tears. I hadn't heard that nickname in years! .... I can't believe that I'd just killed my one true friend.

    I stormed back into my room to gain my composure, and stop my arm from bleeding. My arm was sliced open pretty good so it took a while for the bleeding to stop. I couldn't go to the hospital so I did the next best thing, I called Bryant. Twenty minutes later Mr. Johnson was knocking at my door, he brought Lenny with him to patch up my arm. After getting the towel completely unwrapped from my wound Lenny explained that it was worse than he expected and I'd need to have several stitches. While fighting off the tears and flinching from the needle and thread piercing my skin, I starred at my mentor and asked two questions, "I need to ask you something Bryant and please don't lie!" Bryant looked at me with his signature stone faced look and replied "Go ahead!" I continued by asking "Did you train Erica too? because she used the same fighting style that I learned at the gym." He looked me deep into my eyes and calmly said that he hadn't even laid eyes on her before and the only reason he knows of her is because of me and how I opened up to him about her and my time at the orphanage. At first I didn't believe him, but the look in his eyes convinced me that he was starting the truth. With Lenny putting the last cross stitch in my arm I asked both of them what did they truly know about the faculty then filled them in on all the information that I'd been collecting for the last few months. They collectively chimed in to fill in some blanks and offer up other details that I might've been missing. We cleaned up the room and departed one by one. We regrouped at Mr. Johnson's house where Glen was already there putting together a couple of items that I wanted for this last mission. I wanted to be completely below the radar for this job. A week later I received a phone call from an unknown number, I answered but didn't say a word, the voice on the other end simply said "The package you seek will be on the move tomorrow at 6.30 p.m." then hung up. It was finally time!

PRICK

Less than twenty-four hours from now I'll finally be seating face to face with the boss, the head of the faculty, the one who turned my dear friend against me. I believe this might've been the first time that I was extremely eager to do a job, and I know for a fact that this would be the first time that I wouldn't be getting paid for a hit, and I was quite ok with that.

    I woke up the next morning with a different motivation. I always got nervous before a job, but not today, today I was more eager than anything. As noon struck the clock I started to do my make-up and by two-thirty I was getting dressed. In order for me to pull this off I'd have to be flawless with my every move, I asked Mr. Johnson to get me an older car that'll match my disguise and also a cane. My target would be at the southwest terminal at gate four, but I had no idea if they would be traveling alone or not, for this reason I planned on getting there early. I headed out on my twenty minute drive at four fifty on the dot and was at the gate seated by five twenty. At a quarter to six I spotted my target approaching the seating area walking through the crowd with shades on and a scarf unknowing that this will be the last few moments of their life. Acting as if I was dozing off I heard a familiar voice asking if the seat next to me was taken. Being full of rage I had to calm myself before shaking my head and a hand wave as to motion to go right ahead. I struck up a conversation mostly about nothing, but making sure that my victim wouldn't move. At six fifteen sharp the announcement blared over the loud speaker "we'll start

The Hansom Hustla

boarding flight eight thirty-four to Cancun shortly" "Check your surroundings to make sure you gathered all your belongings and get ready for loading". Everyone hustled and shuffled around gathering their belongings anticipating the boarding call as my victim leaned over to express their excitement of finally retiring and going on their dream vacation then the announcement came. "We will be allowing the seniors and person's with children that are flying first class to board first then everyone else in first class will be called next". My victim rose from their seat and turned to me saying "I guess I'll see you when we land", "It was nice talking to you" as they reached out to shake my hand. I got up from my seat with my arms out saying "give me a hug! I know that we've only spoke for a short time, but it feels like I've known you forever." They smiled and said that for some strange reason they felt the same way, leaned in for the hug and as I patted them on the back, poking them with a new thumb tack with every with every pat, I whispered in their ear "Rest in hell Edna Burke" then took my cane and hobbled off leaving her with the most startling look on her face. She fell back in the chair lost for words as I slowly disappeared into the crowd.

www.ingramcontent.com/pod-product-compliance
Lightning Source LLC
LaVergne TN
LVHW092058060526
838201LV00047B/1444